Imagine you're a
Tairy!

First published in
paperback in 2003 by
Zero To Ten,
part of Evans Brothers Limited,
2A Portman Mansions, Chiltern St, London W1U 6NR

Reprinted 2005

Publisher: Anna McQuinn
Art Director: Tim Foster
Senior Editor: Simona Sideri
Publishing Assistant: Vikram Parashar

A CIP catalogue record for this book is available
from the British Library.

ISBN 1-84089-280-3

Printed in China

Imagine you're a
Fairy!

Magic Meg
used to live in the Enchanted Forest where
she taught fledgling fairies, pixies and elves to read
runes and write the magic alphabet. The most
important lessons she taught were how to fly on
moonbeams and gossamer into the land of dreams.

Lucy Loveheart
has a special interest in fairies. She is particularly
fascinated by the Enchanted Forest and spends
much of her time daydreaming about it. She works
mainly in watercolour, collage, stickers and glitter,
but she also uses a little bit of magic and fairy dust.

We would like to dedicate this book to three wonderful fairy godmothers:

Joan, Connie and Mary.

What is a fairy?

It is very difficult to describe
fairies because they are made out of
the imagination, not out of words.
Human beings very rarely meet fairies
but those who have say that:
Fairies are usually smaller than humans.
Fairies are very secret.
Fairies live in an enchanted world.
Fairies do magic.

What do fairies look like?

There are lots of different kinds of fairies.

They come in many different shapes and sizes.

Tiara

Regal expression

Good luck charm

Magic wand

Straight back

Wings

Stars and fairy dust

Flying shoes

Whatever they look like, all fairies are very clever and very magical.

Different types of fairies

Brownies: *very kindly*

Pixies: *very fast and lively*

Goblins: *ugly little demons but clever*

Sprites: *almost invisible*

Gnomes: *live underground*

Not all fairies are pretty, with gauzy, rainbow wings and frilly frocks. Some are rough and tough and very naughty. Some are spiteful and many of them are ugly and have no kind of dress sense. Here are some of the other types.

Imps: *very naughty*

Elves: *mischievous, but good leaders*

Tooth fairies: *like living near humans*

Boggarts and bugganes: *bad tempered*

Banshees: *female and scream a lot*

Leprechauns

They live in Ireland and look like very small old men. They like drinking a drink called poteen, which makes them rather spiteful. They guard treasure buried in pots and hide it at the end of rainbows. They carry two purses, one with a magic coin and one with fools' gold.

Will o' the wisps
(Jack-muh-lantern in the U.S.A.)
They live in swamps and marshes and lure humans into them with elf-fire.

The little people
They live in the Isle of Man, where people still believe in fairies. They wear red caps and green jackets and hunt with multi-coloured hounds.

Where do fairies live?

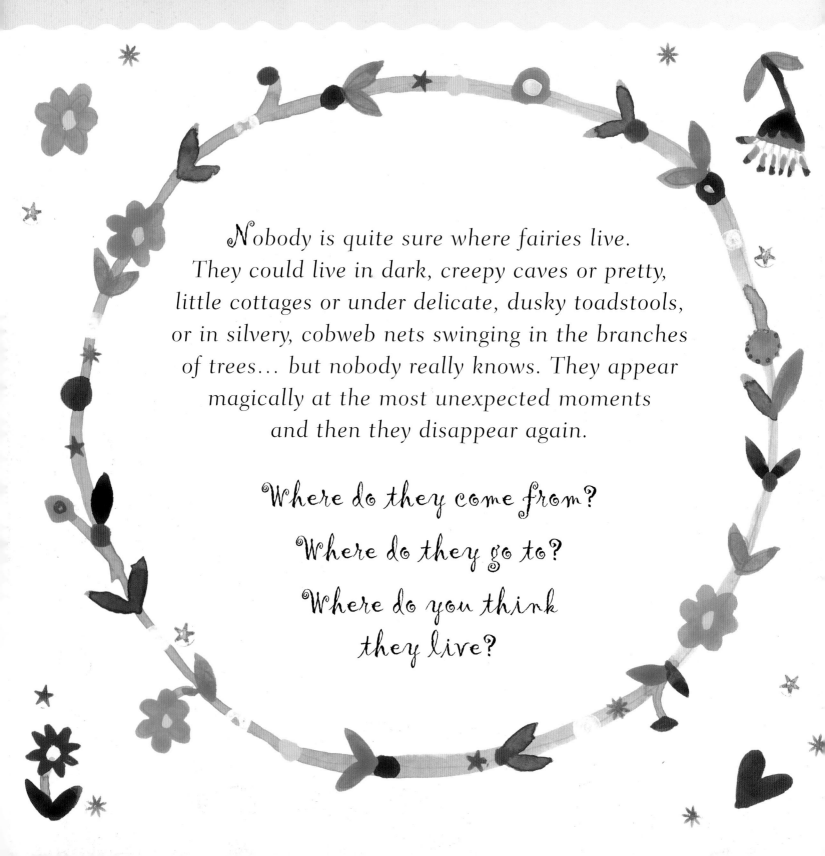

Nobody is quite sure where fairies live. They could live in dark, creepy caves or pretty, little cottages or under delicate, dusky toadstools, or in silvery, cobweb nets swinging in the branches of trees… but nobody really knows. They appear magically at the most unexpected moments and then they disappear again.

Where do they come from?
Where do they go to?
Where do you think they live?

Outfits and clothes

Fairies need special outfits for special occasions.

Disguise

Casual outfit

Magic-making outfit

Party outfit

Equipment and accessories

Fairies need special accessories to help
them with their work.

Magic wands

Handbag

Flying shoes

Cloak of invisibility

Book of spells

Magic potion

Fairy dust

Flower fairy pollen

Nectar of toadstools

Wings

Tiaras

Glitter

Magic and spells

Fairies can do lots of magical things,
like flying, appearing and disappearing,
and making dreams come true. In order to
do magic it is essential to have a wand,
some wings, some fairy dust, a tiara
(or a baseball cap will do) and a book of spells.
A fairy's book of spells is very special
and very secret but here are some examples
of typical fairy spells.

Secret spell n.115

Magic spell for good luck

You will need:

1 cup of daisy heads

2 spoonfuls of rosebuds

8 spoonfuls of morning dew

1 four-leaved clover
(a three-leaved clover will sometimes
work if you can't find one)

1 magic wand

1 mixing bowl

Directions

1. Mix the daisy heads, rosebuds
and morning dew in mixing bowl.

2. Place bowl by your feet.

3. Hold clover in your right hand.

4. Hold wand upright in left hand.

5. Close eyes and say,
"Make my dream come true!"

Things that go wrong

Magic is a tricky thing and inexperienced fairies often get it wrong. It has been known for fairies to crash land in bramble bushes because they have not taken enough care of their wings. Fairy dust has a nasty habit of making you sneeze. It is very awkward to appear magically in the wrong place at the wrong time. Even worse is when a magic spell makes a nightmare come true instead of a lovely dream. Not all fairies are good. Some are rather bad and they make things go wrong on purpose.

Secret spell n.409

Magic spell for general mischief

You will need:

1 cup of water

3 old conkers (or acorns)

1 handful of playground dust

2 pieces of sticky tape

1 spoonful of earth

4 old oak leaves

Directions

Place all the ingredients into an old tin at dead of night (around 9 o'clock). Use wand in position A (see page about Wand Practice). Shout, "Banshee! Banshee!" and spell will be effective.

Wand practice

Hold wand firmly in hand. Smooth action.
Concentration essential.

Polish wand after use.
Keep in a safe place.

A. Making magic spells

B. Turning frogs into princes

C. Making dreams come true

D. Blowing fairy dust everywhere.

Flying practice

For best results do
flying practice unobserved.
Avoid built-up areas.
Always aim for
smooth landing.

A. *The flutter position*

B. Swooping upwards

**Polish wings with fairy dust after use.
Hang up in fairy wardrobe.**

D. Gliding

C. *Butterfly flying*

Fairy godmothers

These are special fairies because they come in human form. A fairy godmother can be young or middle-aged, but the favourite sort of fairy godmother is quite old, with a wrinkly face and a lovely encouraging smile.

Fairy godmothers are invited to lots of their godchildren's birthday parties. The children's parents expect special presents such as health, kindness, bravery, patience, cheerfulness, obedience and good fortune… but the children would rather have toys or chocolate.

At the moment there are not many fairy godfathers, but this is considered to be very unfair and the Fairy Union (F.U.N.) is looking into it because there is a great demand for good fairy godfathers.

The Fairy Union (F.U.N.)

The Fairy Union (F.U.N.) insists that all fairies follow a strict code of conduct and obey the rules for fairies.

Rules

1. Always carry your wand although it may be disguised as something else under certain circumstances.

2. Always be on the look out for wicked witches who may cast horrid spells.

3. Look after your wings properly. Hang them up before you go to bed at night and polish them with fairy dust once a week.

4. Never stick out your tongue at a fairy godmother or the fairy king or you may get turned into a pumpkin.

Motto: Imagine magic and make believe

The Enchanted Forest

1. Gossamer clouds – *dreams come true when you sleep in these.*

2. Tooth fairy factory – *tooth fairies collect children's baby teeth when they fall out and grind them down very finely to use in fairy dust.*

3. Stars – *used in dreams and for making glitter.*

4. Flying school – *all young fairies must attend.*

5. Store cupboard – *safe storage for magic dust.*

6. Wing polishers – *a specially-trained team of elves to polish fairies' wings.*

7. **Boutique** – where fairies buy designer outfits.
8. **Wand shop** – for new wands and repairs.
9. **Fairy ring** – the fairies' dancing ground.
10. **Wishing well** –the water from this well is used in magic potions.

11. **Toadstools** – where fairies sit to think or have their homes.
12. **Cobweb cradles** – baby fairies never cry when they are rocked in these.
13. **Allotment** – the fairies' vegetable garden.

Jobs list

1. Wand practice.

2. Prepare potions
to take to sick creatures in the
Enchanted Forest.

3. Water flowers and herbs
in the allotment.

4. Make new magic spells
and practise old ones.

5. Polish wings, wand
and flying shoes.

6. Contact members of F.U.N.
and invite to Moonlight Ball.

7. Make Magic Fairy Bars for tea.

Fairy words

gossamer

pumpkin

wand

disappear

magic

invisible

moon beam

abracadabra

cobwebs

secrets

toadstool

mischief

Although fairies are very good at making spells,
they are not very good at speling. Can you help
them match these pairs of singulars and plurals.

fairy tooth	elf bushes	cradle shoe
tiara fairies	disguises bush	shoes labels
teeth tiaras	elves disguise	label cradles

How many new words can you spell from the letters in
Enchanted Forest?

Famous fairies

Tinkerbell

Tinkerbell is a pretty little fairy who lives in Never Never land. This is in the story of Peter Pan by J.M. Barrie. She has great fun with Peter Pan and the Lost Boys, until a girl called Wendy comes to live there too. Tinkerbell is so jealous that she causes a great deal of mischief and nearly loses her magical powers before everything turns out well in the end.

Titania, Oberon and Puck

These are famous fairies in a play called A Midsummer Night's Dream by William Shakespeare. Titania is the very beautiful Queen of the Fairies and Oberon is the powerful King of the Fairies. All through the play they weave magic spells with the help of their cunning little fairy servant, called Puck, who makes life very difficult for a lot of people. This story turns out well in the end too. Thank goodness.

Famous fairy godmothers

The most famous fairy
godmothers appear in the stories
of Cinderella and The Sleeping Beauty.
In both stories the beautiful heroines need
a lot of help from their fairy godmothers.
Cinderella needs a coach, a new pair of glass
slippers, a handsome prince, a designer ball gown
and goodness knows what else. She is saved from
a life of housework by her very kind godmother.

The Sleeping Beauty is imprisoned inside a rose
bush and would still be there if her fairy
godmother had not arranged for a passing
prince to cut her out and wake her up
with a kiss. This must have been
rather a shock for her.

Things to do

Fairy dust

Fairy dust helps to make magic properly.
Make your own fairy dust by mixing together:

1 pinch of silver glitter

1 pinch of gold glitter

1 pinch of small sequins

Put together in a little bottle marked fairy dust.
Use sparingly and sprinkle wherever
and whenever needed.

Make a crown

Cut a strip of silver paper big enough to
wrap around your head. Glue the ends together
and decorate with magic shapes of your choice.

Make a wand

Wands make things appear and disappear
and are very good for helping spells. To make
your own, cut out a large star shape
and decorate with glitter, stars and hearts.
Attach this to a long stick painted in
the colour of your choice.

Fairy bars

You will need:

75g margarine or butter

75g breakfast cereal (flakes or crispy rice)

1 tablespoon syrup

2 chocolate bars

Fresh flowers to decorate

Directions

Place margarine or butter into saucepan. Add chocolate bars and syrup. Melt on low heat. Turn off heat and stir cereal in until coated. Put onto greased tray and when almost cool cut into bars. Arrange bars onto pretty plate and decorate with flower petals. (Watch them disappear like magic!)

Practise flying

You'll need wings first. Make your wings by cutting out a piece of net or shimmery material into wing shapes. Ask your fairy godmother to help you. Then decorate with star and heart shapes and glitter. Only a few very special fairies can really fly, but if you run or skip around the garden and flap your arms up and down with wings attached it almost feels like flying.